The Letter

T0315345

VISTA®
HIGHER LEARNING

Boston, Massachusetts

SOCIAL STUDIES

Gustavo is 15 years old. He lives in a small town in New York. His family is from Caracas, Venezuela.

Gustavo loves reading. He often goes to the library after school. He reads all kinds of books there. He has been going to the library since he was little. He always feels very happy there.

Gustavo has a good imagination. It's easy for him to see pictures and ideas in his mind.

However, Gustavo's friends don't read many books. Instead, they watch videos and play games alone on their phones. They don't go to the library.

Gustavo doesn't understand. When he reads, he uses his imagination. He learns lots of new things. "Books are fun!" he thinks. He wants his friends to like books, too.

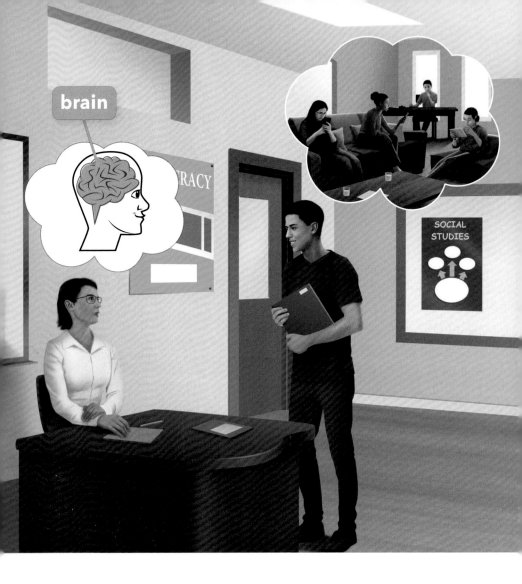

Gustavo talks to his Social Studies teacher, Mrs. Vega. He tells her about his friends.

"They don't like reading?" she asks in surprise. "That's too bad. Reading books is really important," she explains. "It's good for your brain. It helps you learn new words. It helps you remember things better, too."

"I have some ideas to get my friends to read more," says Gustavo. "But I'm just a teenager. What can I do?"

Mrs. Vega thinks for a moment. "You should tell your ideas to the **city council**. They're a group of city **politicians**. Their job is to listen to **citizens'** ideas. They work with the **mayor**. They help the **community**."

"Good idea!" says Gustavo. "Do you have their phone number?"

Mrs. Vega thinks again. "I think it's best if you write them a letter," she explains.

A city council is a type of **government**. The mayor is the **leader**. The council members are **representatives** for the citizens. They **are elected** by the people of a city. They make **laws** and offer services to the **local** community. They do things like build parks and start **programs** for the community.

After school, Gustavo goes to the library. He reads about the city council.

Gustavo isn't sure what to do. Can he really make a difference? He almost gives up. Then, he remembers Mrs. Vega's advice. "I'll send my idea to the council," he thinks. "Maybe they *can* help me. I won't know unless I try."

Gustavo takes out his favorite pen and some notebook paper. He starts writing his letter.

Gustavo almost gives up. He almost stops trying.

KNOW IT ALL

Writing with pen and paper is better sometimes. It makes you think more. This can make your writing clearer. It can also help you think of ideas.

activity center

Dear City Council,

My name is Gustavo González and I'm 15 years old. I'm writing to you about a problem. Teens do not read a lot today. I have ideas to change that. We could have a new program at the library. Teenagers would read books to children. The teens would get points for each book they read. They could get gifts for points. It would be a great way to get more young people reading!

I have another idea, too. My friends and most teenagers use their phones too much. I think it's because they don't have other fun things to do. I want to make an **activity center**. It would be a special place just for teenagers. They could play games, do sports, talk, and have fun. Thank you for reading my letter.

Sincerely,

Gustavo González

Gustavo mails the letter and waits to see what will happen. Two weeks later, his mom comes to his room. "Gustavo!" she says with a smile. "There's a letter for you! It looks important."

Gustavo opens the letter. He gets a surprised look on his face.

"What is it?" asks his mom.

Gustavo shows his mom the letter. "It's a letter from the mayor!" he explains.

Gustavo reads the letter carefully. The city council loves his ideas. They think Gustavo may have a good **solution** to the reading problem. They want to hear more from him about his plans!

"Will you come to our next meeting?" they ask.

"Yes!" thinks Gustavo. His mom is proud. Gustavo is happy and really excited, too!

The next month, Gustavo goes to the city council meeting. He wears a nice dress shirt and a tie. He feels a little scared, but he's happy to be there. Mrs. Vega is there, too. She smiles and Gustavo feels better.

A council member says that Gustavo will speak next. He takes a deep breath and walks to the front of the room. He **gives his speech**. He talks about his ideas. As he speaks, he sees that people are smiling. When he finishes, everyone claps for him.

Later, the mayor comes over to Gustavo. "You're a very good speaker," he says. He shakes Gustavo's hand. "We'd like you to be our teen **ambassador**. You can help the council find ways to help teens. Are you interested?"

Gustavo smiles. "Yes!" he answers. "Thank you, that would be amazing! Maybe we can talk to the library next week?"

The mayor smiles and agrees.

Gustavo and the city council tell their ideas to the people at the library. They think it's a great plan.

The library starts using Gustavo's ideas. More teenagers start going to the library. They read lots of books to children and earn points. Both the teenagers and the children have a lot of fun. The library becomes very busy.

Gustavo sees that his friends aren't using their phones as much. He feels proud of his work.

Next, Gustavo and the council find a building near the library. They make it into an activity center. Teens can play games together and have fun. Everyone thinks it's very cool!

Later, Mrs. Vega visits Gustavo at the activity center. "Thank you for the idea," he says. "You helped me a lot."

Mrs. Vega smiles. "You did the work, Gustavo," she says. "You had the idea. You wrote the letter. You spoke at the meeting. You're the one who made our community a better place!"

city council officials at the city level who are chosen by the people and who make decisions for a city or town

politician a member of a group of people chosen to control a city or country

citizen a person who legally lives in a country or city and has certain rights

mayor the highest official in a city who is chosen by the people

community a group of people who are connected by geography, culture, or interest

government the group that controls a nation, state, or city

leader a person who controls or manages a group of people and guides them

representative a person who speaks and acts for for a specific group

be elected to be chosen by the people of a group for an office or position

law a rule made by the people in control of a city or country that says what people can or cannot do

local in an area close to something

program a special activity designed to help or educate

activity center a place to get together with other people to play games or do other things for fun or enjoyment

solution the answer to a problem

give a speech to speak to a group of people, usually for a special event or for a certain reason

ambassador a person who speaks to others and acts for a country, city, or group